MW00901767

Sam,

Where do I begin?! I could have never guessed how our relationship would develop back when we first met at that board meeting. We've had some great times together from sitting courtside, ToneHouse at 5am on a Monday to taking tequila shots! By ~~knowing~~ having you in my life I have become a better person. You have taught me to always be confident and more importantly to remember never take life too seriously and always smile as well as "you probably should have one more drink". You are one of the most genuine souls I have ever come across in my entire life, I am blessed to have you in my life. I ~~want~~ hope you have the best time abroad, I am so excited for you and the adventure that lays ahead. If you ever make it back to the US, what do say we grab that drink?

"Big"

Milo And Shiloh's Big Move

By Peter De Jianne

Illustrated by Heather Workman

Milo and Shiloh's Big Move

Illustrator and page layout: Heather Workman
Editor: Bobbie Hinman

ISBN: 978-0-692-14647-7
Library of Congress Control Number: 2018908256

Peter De Jianne
www.booksbypdj.com

This book is dedicated to my twin brother Thomas.
Thank you for always being there for me,
and more importantly for always being my best friend.

And to any child who has ever been bullied,
always believe in yourself. You are an incredible person and
will grow up to achieve great success.

-Peter

Milo and Shiloh are twin brothers. They used to live far, far away on Planet Burke with their Mama, Papa, and big brother, Lionel. Every day on Planet Burke was a new adventure.

They climbed hills with their friends and watched the stars in the sky. They played soccer and basketball, and zoomed around the planet on super-fast space scooters.

Milo was always busy building forts out of rocks.

Shiloh kept busy checking the time on his big, shiny space watch to make sure they both made it home before dark.

One night when Papa was tucking Milo and Shiloh into bed, he said, "Boys, I have a special surprise. We are going to be moving to a new home on Planet Kronos!"

The boys were excited. They had heard that Planet Kronos has an orange sky—an orange sky! They would miss their friends, but this was going to be a great, new adventure!

The next day, the family packed their bags and took off for Planet Kronos. Big brother Lionel drove the spaceship. While whizzing along, Papa told the family that the air would feel different on Planet Kronos.

They would all have to wear special masks to help them breathe. "What fun!" thought the boys.

Planet Kronos looked so different from Planet Burke.
The mountains were bigger and seemed to touch the sky.

There were trees with apples the size of watermelons, and the sky really WAS bright orange! Adventures would be so much fun on this new planet.

But Milo and Shiloh had one problem. When they tried to make new friends, they were teased about their masks. The other children didn't wear masks because they were already used to the air on Planet Kronos.

They pointed their fingers at Milo and Shiloh and laughed at them, making them feel sad and lonely. Now they would have to go on adventures all by themselves. They missed their friends on Planet Burke.

One night after dinner, Mama noticed that Milo and Shiloh looked very sad. She asked, "What's wrong, boys? Why are you so unhappy?"

They told Mama that no one wanted to play with them. "They make fun of us because our masks make us look different from the other kids," said Milo.

Mama smiled and said, "Don't listen to what other people say about you. Just listen to the people who care about you. Being different is OK. That's what makes you special."

Then she looked at her boys and said to each one, "There is only one of you in the whole, wide world and each of you needs to be the special person you were meant to be!"

Milo and Shiloh listened to Mama's advice and tried not to pay attention to the teasing. The two of them did all the things they saw the other children doing.

They climbed trees and hung swings from the branches. They built little mountains of rocks.

The other children followed them, watching carefully.

But still calling them names like Mask-Face and Space-Kid.
Then Milo had an idea...

He said, "Let's play the games we played on Planet Burke. Maybe we can teach these kids the games WE love to play." "Great idea," said Shiloh. So they kicked their soccer ball around, played catch with their baseball and took turns throwing a frisbee high in the air.

Then they raced around on their scooters, flying up and down the hills. They laughed and played all day.

The other children watched with wide eyes and began to smile. They only knew how to climb hills, hike up and down the mountains, and build forts. But now they could see how much fun Milo and Shiloh were having playing their games. They wanted to play, too.

"We're so sorry," one of the children said to Milo and Shiloh.
"We're sorry we called you Mask-Face," one shouted.
"Can we play the new games with you?" asked another.

"Yes, of course!" Milo and Shiloh said together. They were so happy to have new friends, and finally felt like they belonged on their new planet.

They would never be lonely again. From now on they would play with their new friends every day.

Mama was right!

"Being different is OK! Always be the special person YOU were meant to be!"
6:15
TIME
FOR
DINNER

CPSIA information can be obtained at www.ICGtesting.com
Printed in the USA
BVIW12n0221300818
525973BV00003B/3

* 9 7 8 0 6 9 2 1 4 6 4 7 7 *